One Day with Big and Little Elly

Written by RP Mickelson
Illustrated by Penny E. Ross

Filidh Publishing

One Day with Big and Little Elly,
Written by RP Mickelson, Illustrated by Penny E. Ross

ISBN 978-1-998307-08-1

Filidh Publishing Corp. Victoria, British Columbia

Cover Art by Penny E. Ross
Manuscript Development and Cover Design by Zoe Duff

Contact the author or the illustrator to order copies:
RP Mickelson (email) rick.mickelson@telus.net
Penny R. Ross (email) pennyross@outlook.com

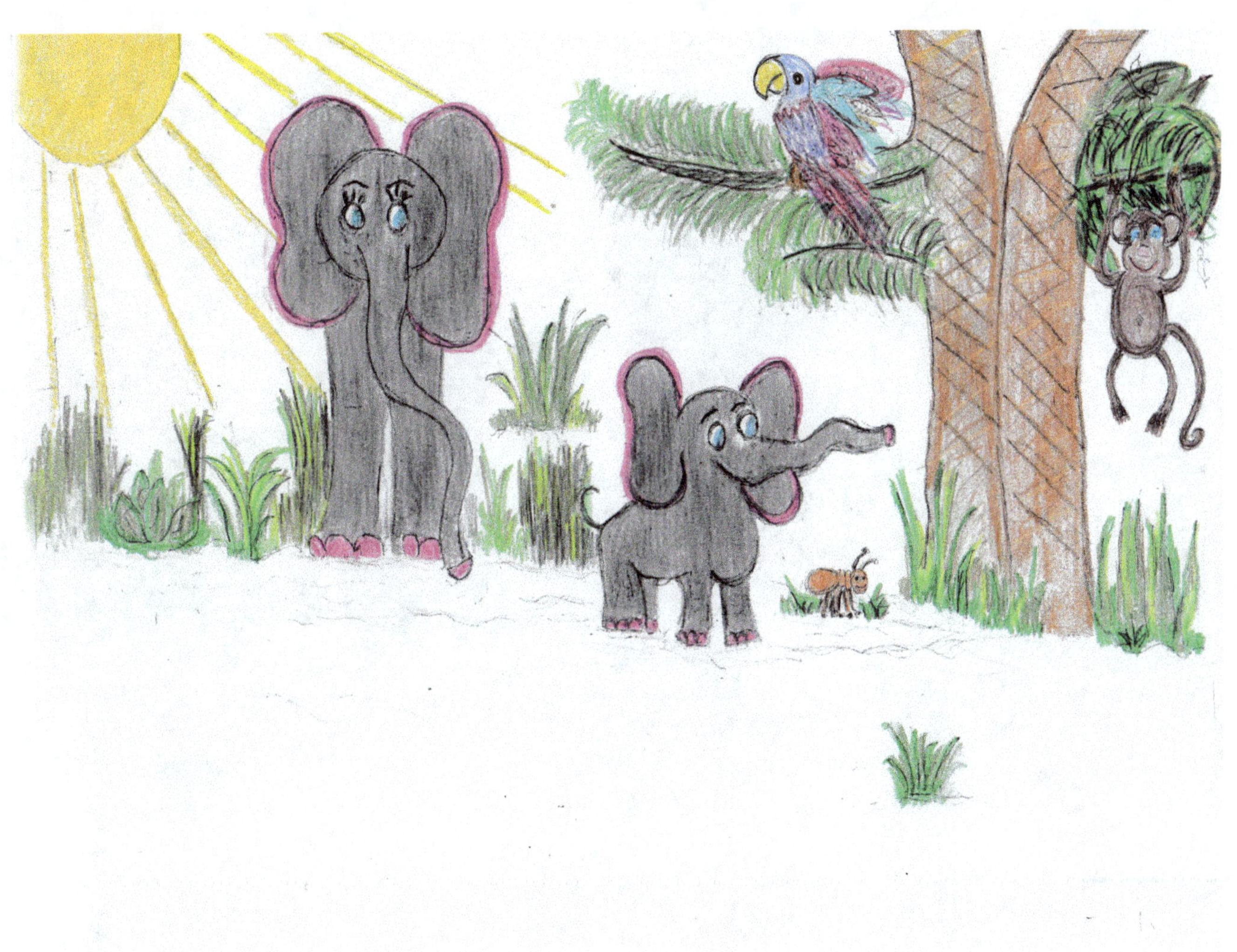

"Look, Mama! There's a parrot in that tree!" said Little Elly.

I can smell it, but I can't see it, Little Elly," said Big Elly."

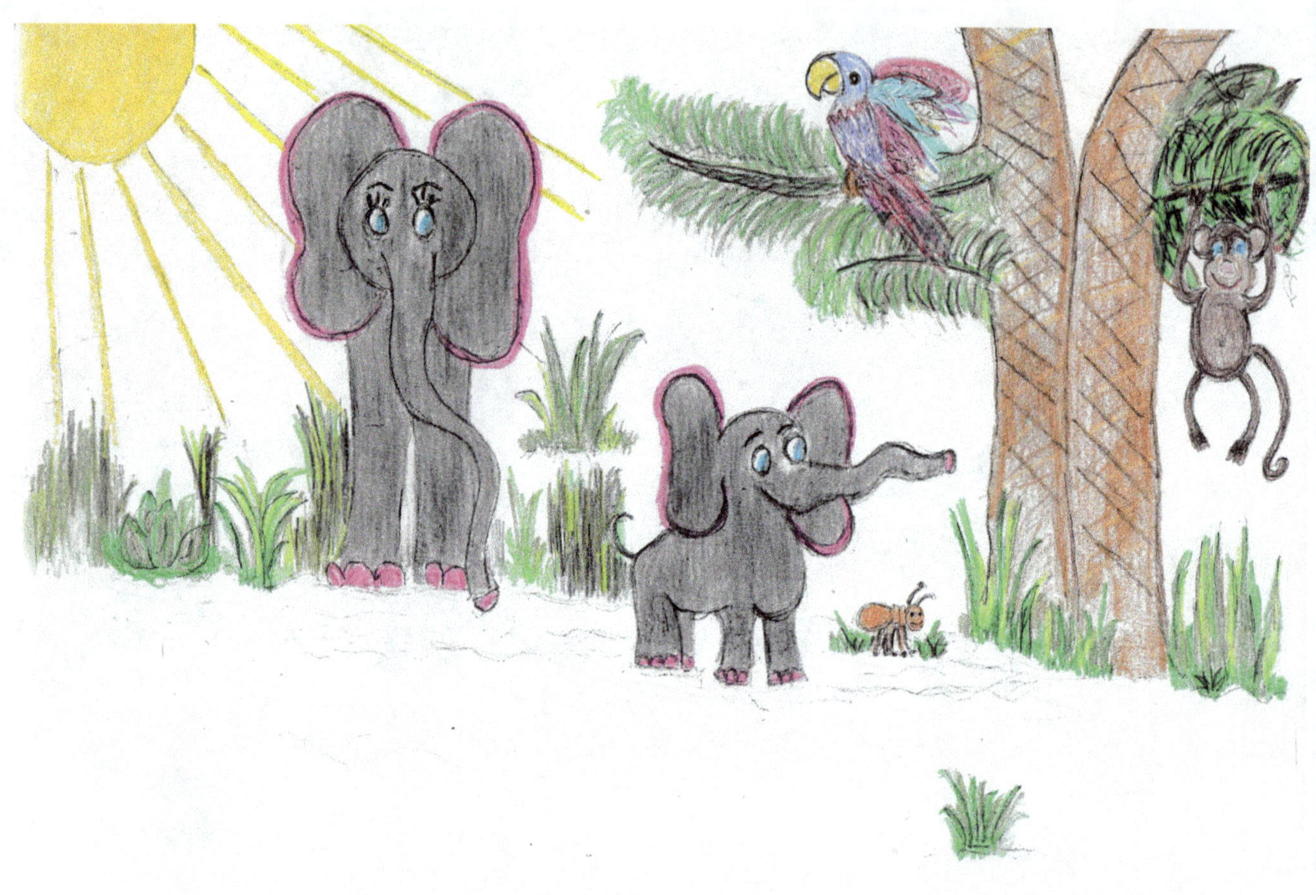

Big Elly then turned toward the tree.

"Can you see it now?" asked Little Elly.

"Yes, I can," said Big Elly.

"Can you see the brown monkey?" asked Little Elly.

"Yes, I can," said Big Elly.

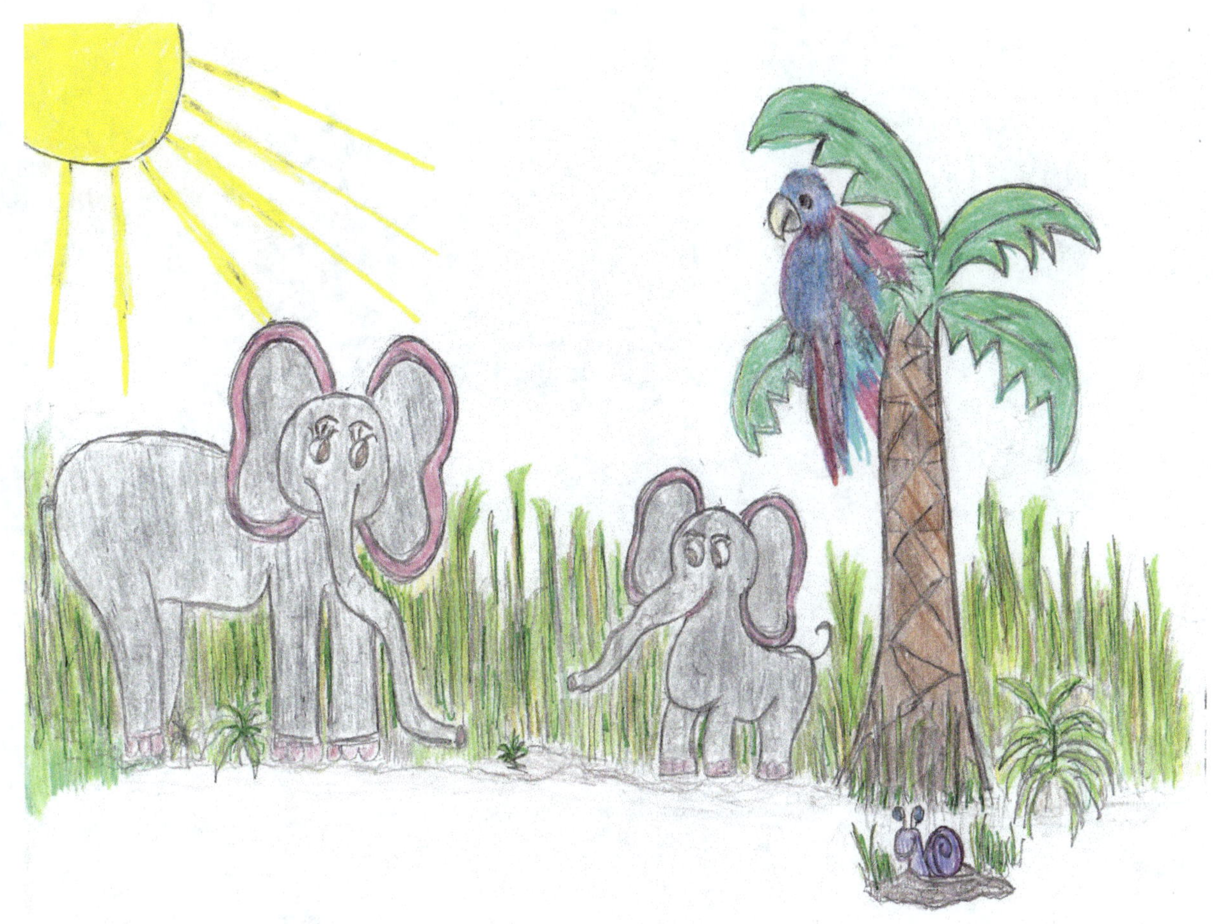

"Can you see the purple slug beside the tree?" asked Little Elly.

"Yes, I can," said Big Elly.

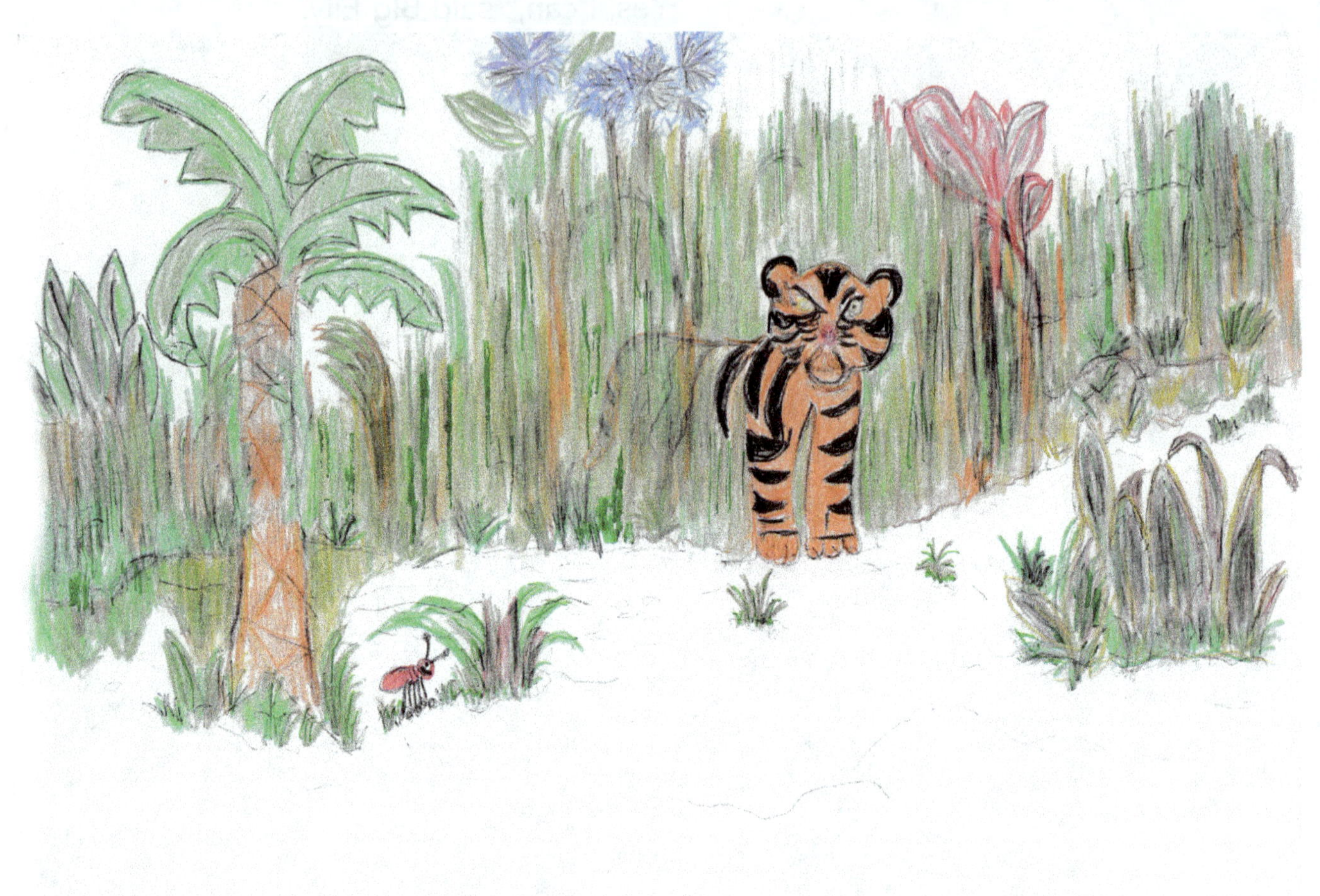

"I smell a baby elephant," growled Tiggy, the tiger.
"And I'm hungry."

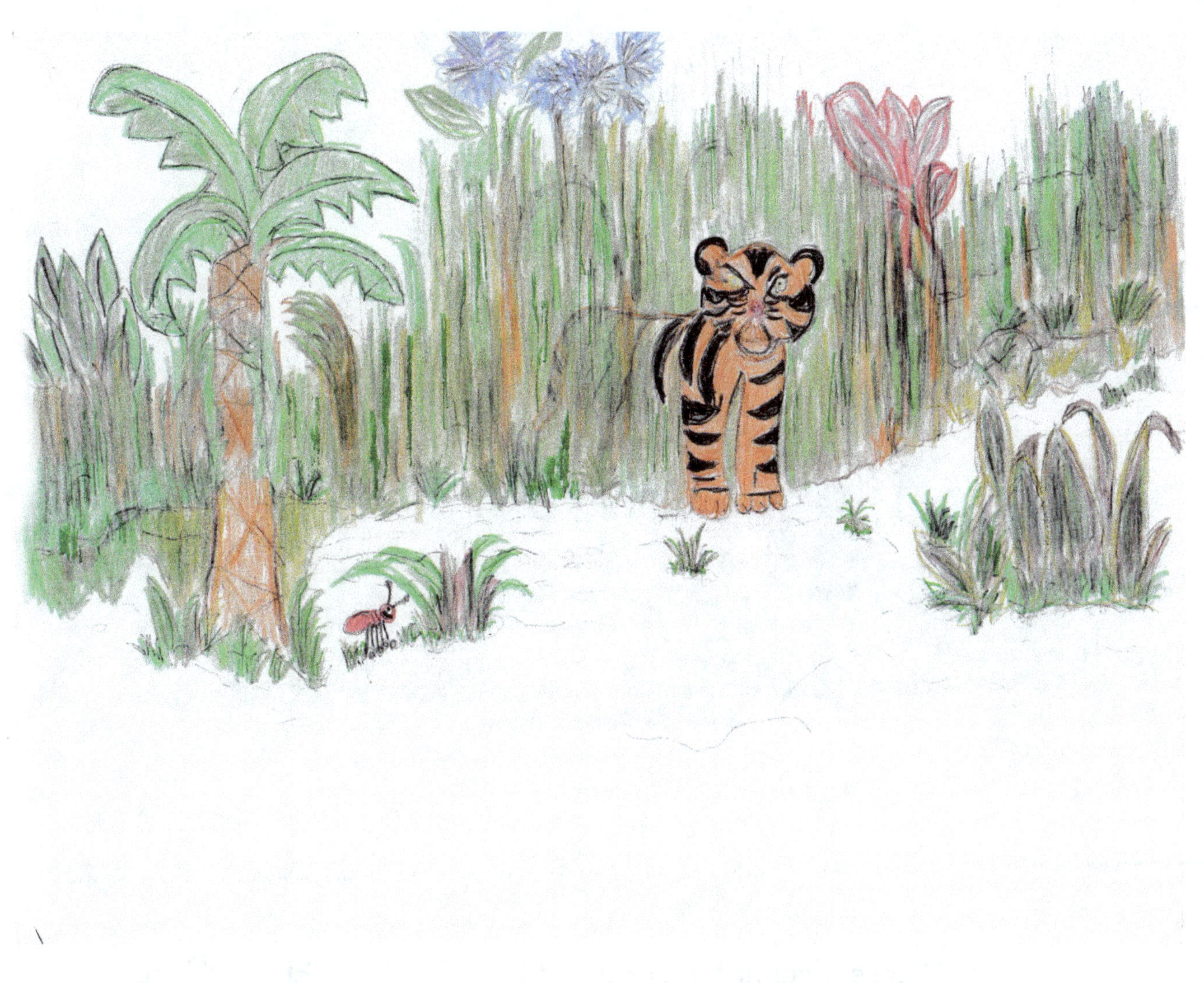

If it is a baby elephant, I'm going to eat it." Tiggy decided.

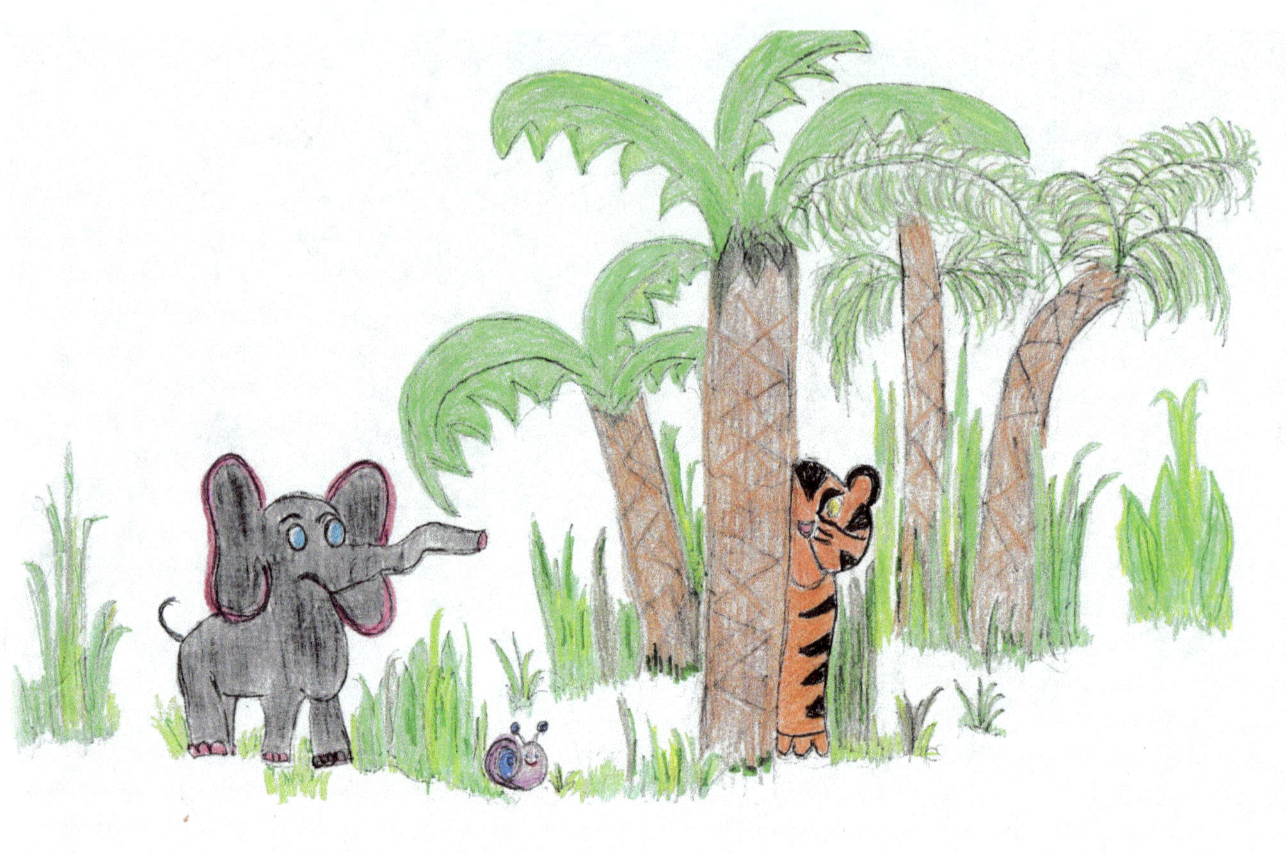

“There's a hungry tiger behind that tree, Little Elly,” whispered Sammy the slug.

“Could it eat me?” replied Little Elly.

“Yes, it could,” said Sammy.

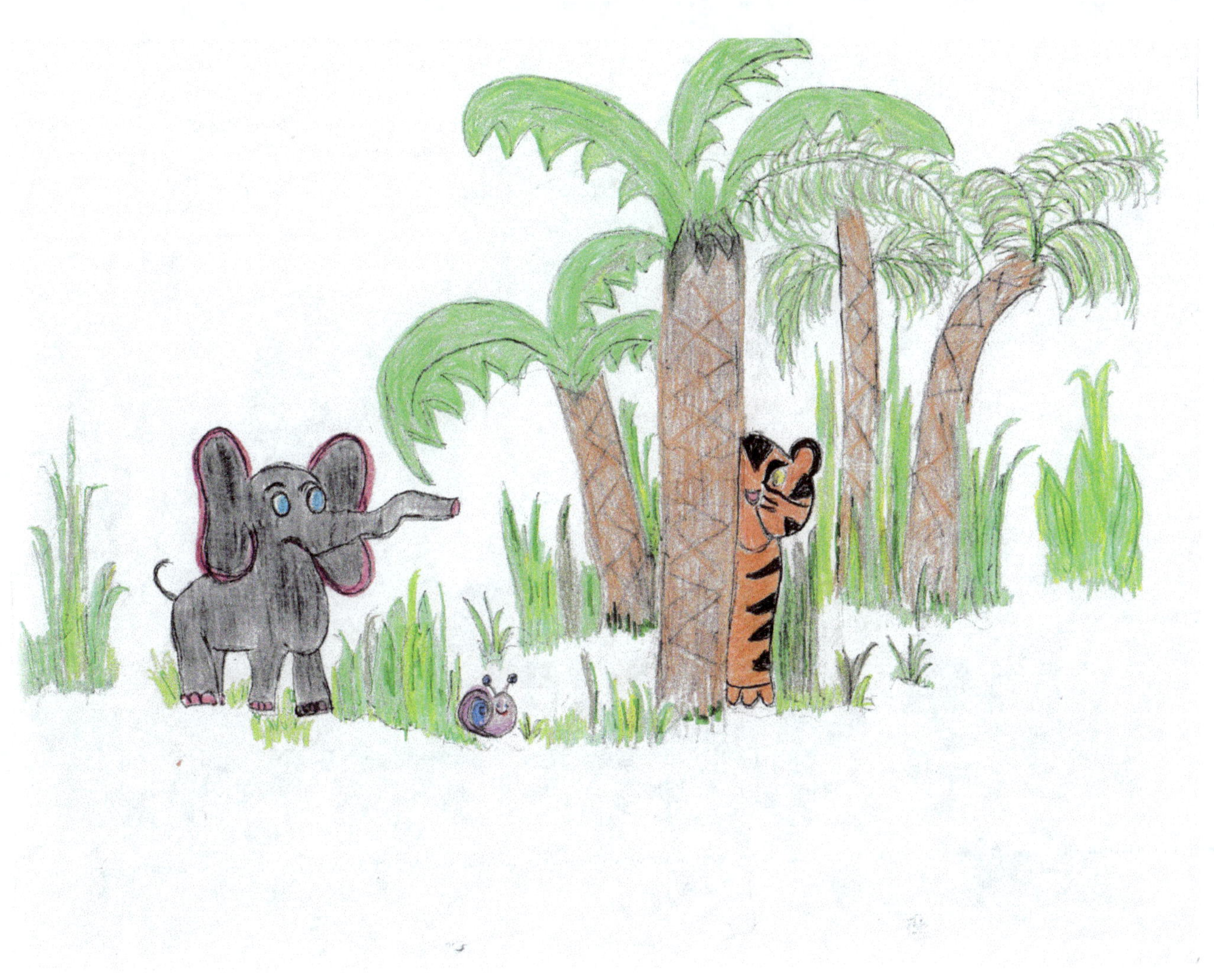

“I can smell that tiger, Sammy, and I can hear it growling,” said Little Elly.

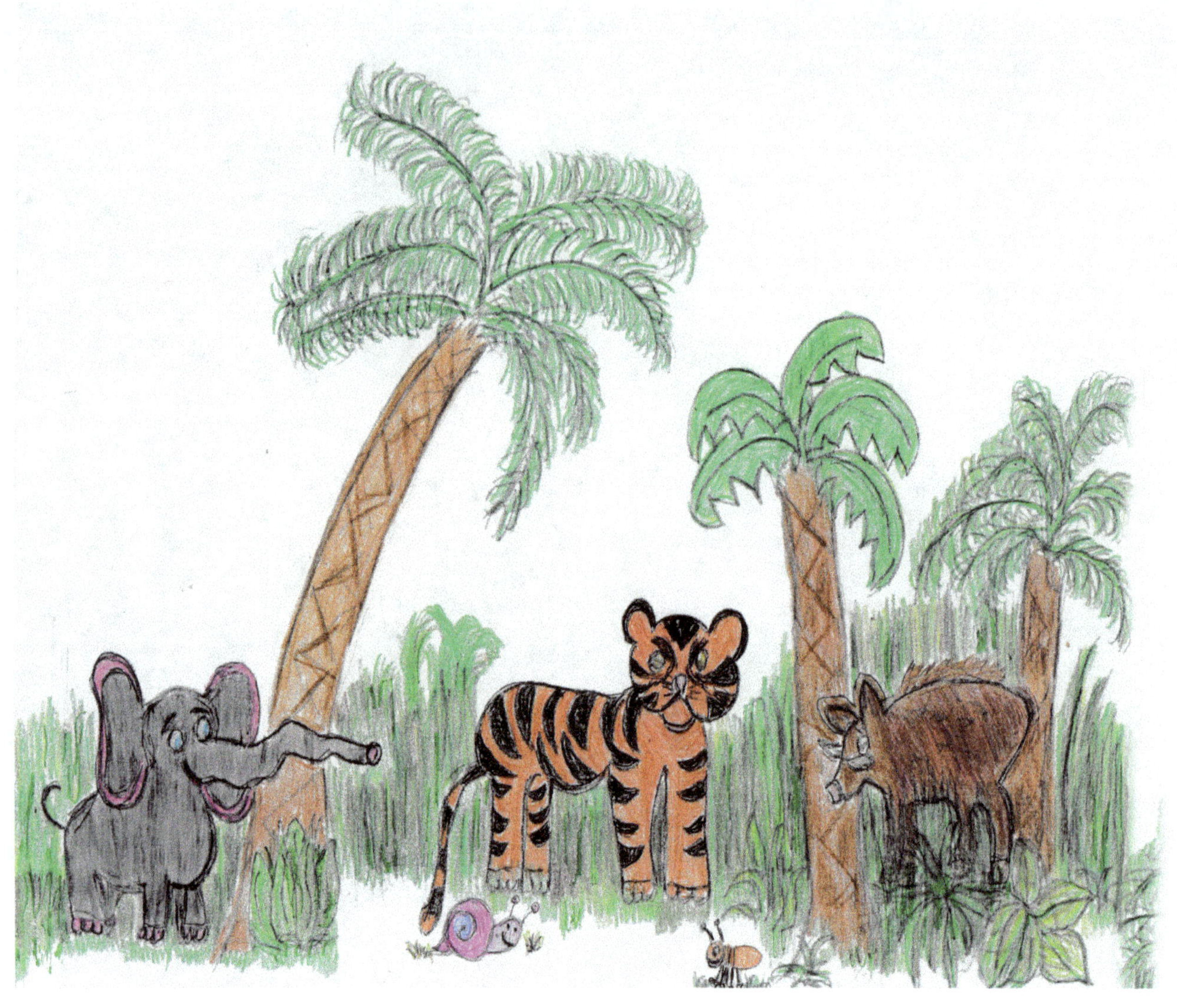

Do you want me to chase Tiggy, the tiger, away from you?" screamed

Billy, the wild boar.

"Yes, I do!" answered Little Elly.

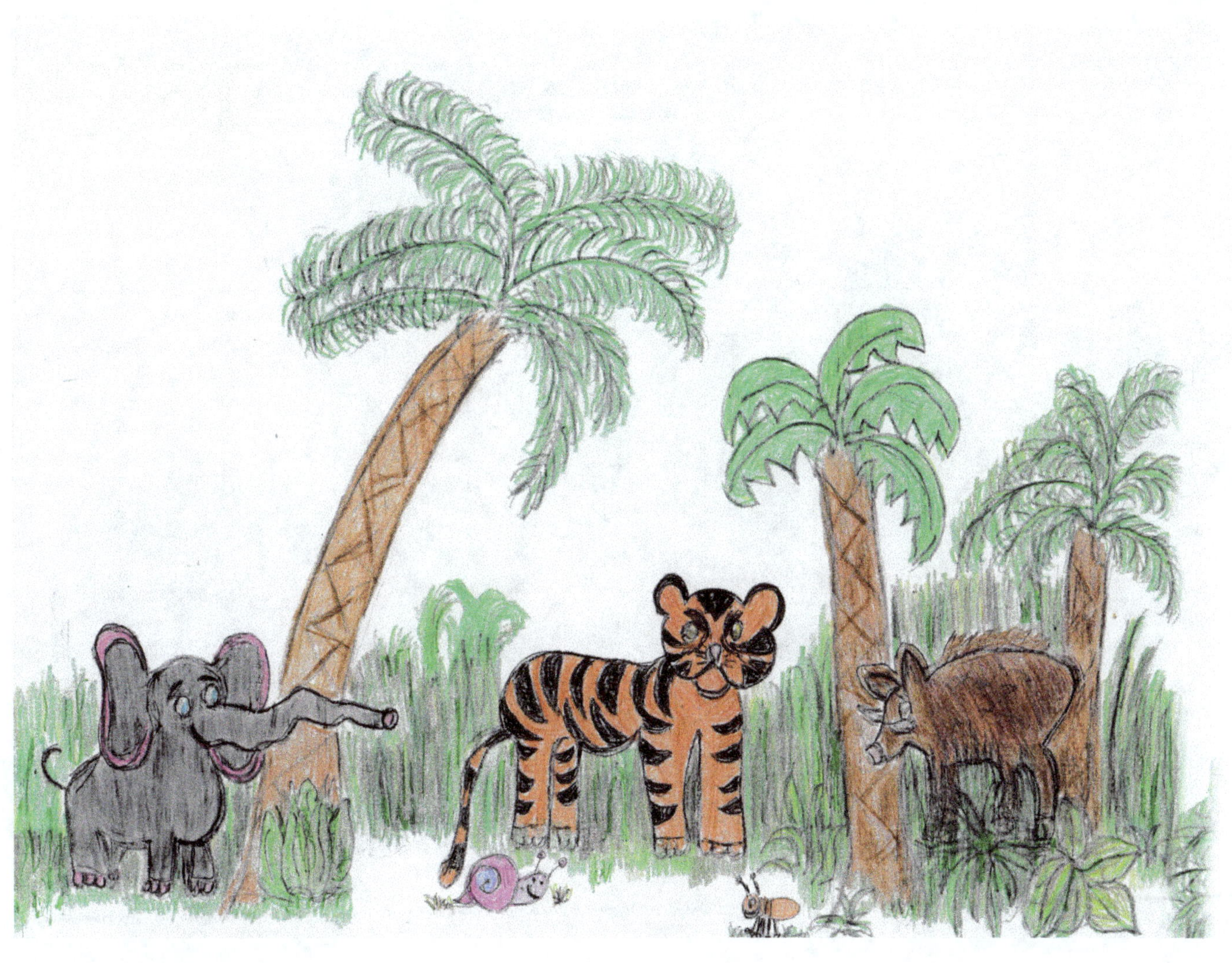

Run away, Tiggy, or I will bite your legs," bellowed Billy.

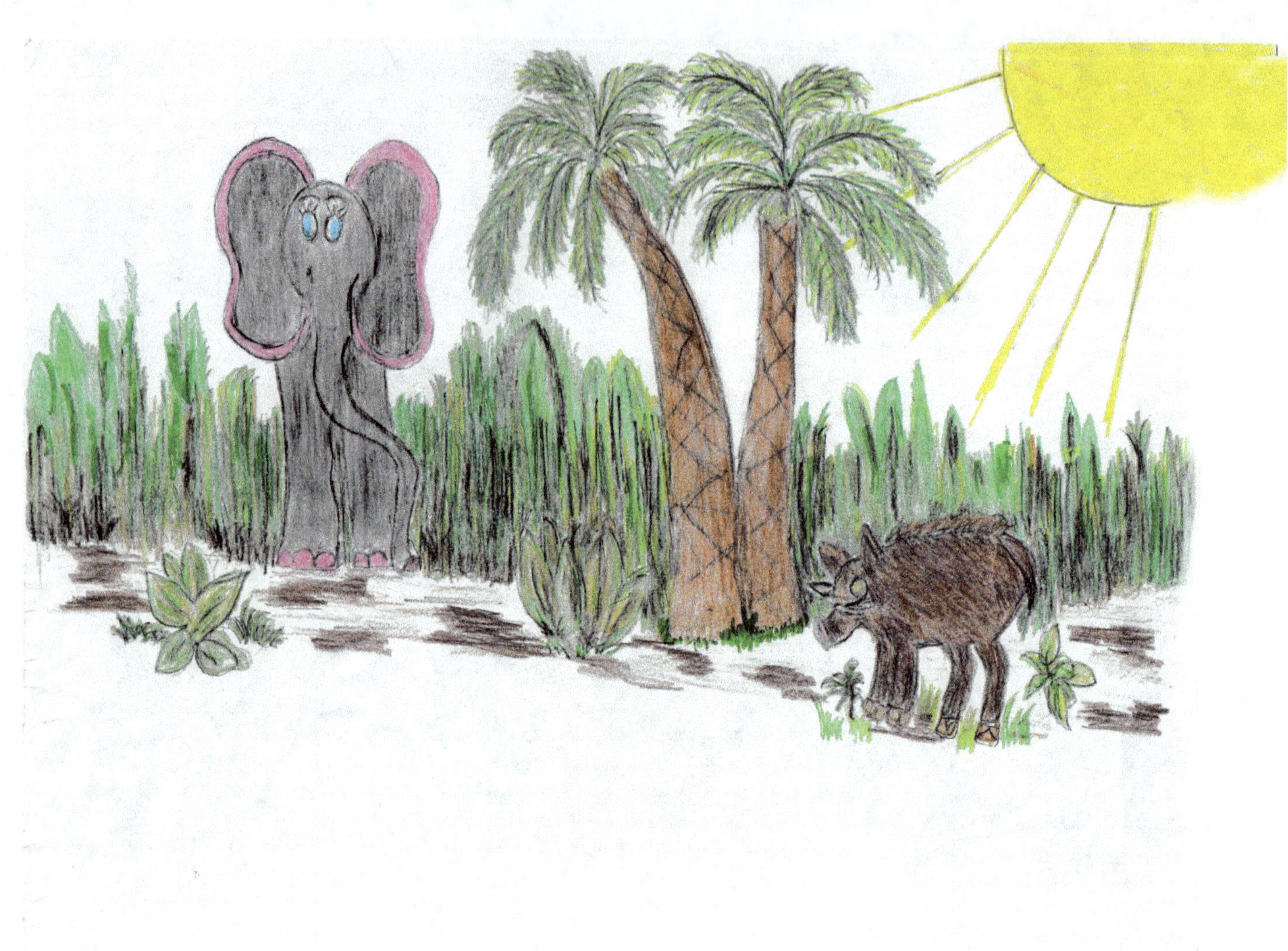

"Tiggy, the tiger is gone now, Little Elly, so you can relax," said Billy.

"Thank you for chasing him away, Billy," replied Little Elly.

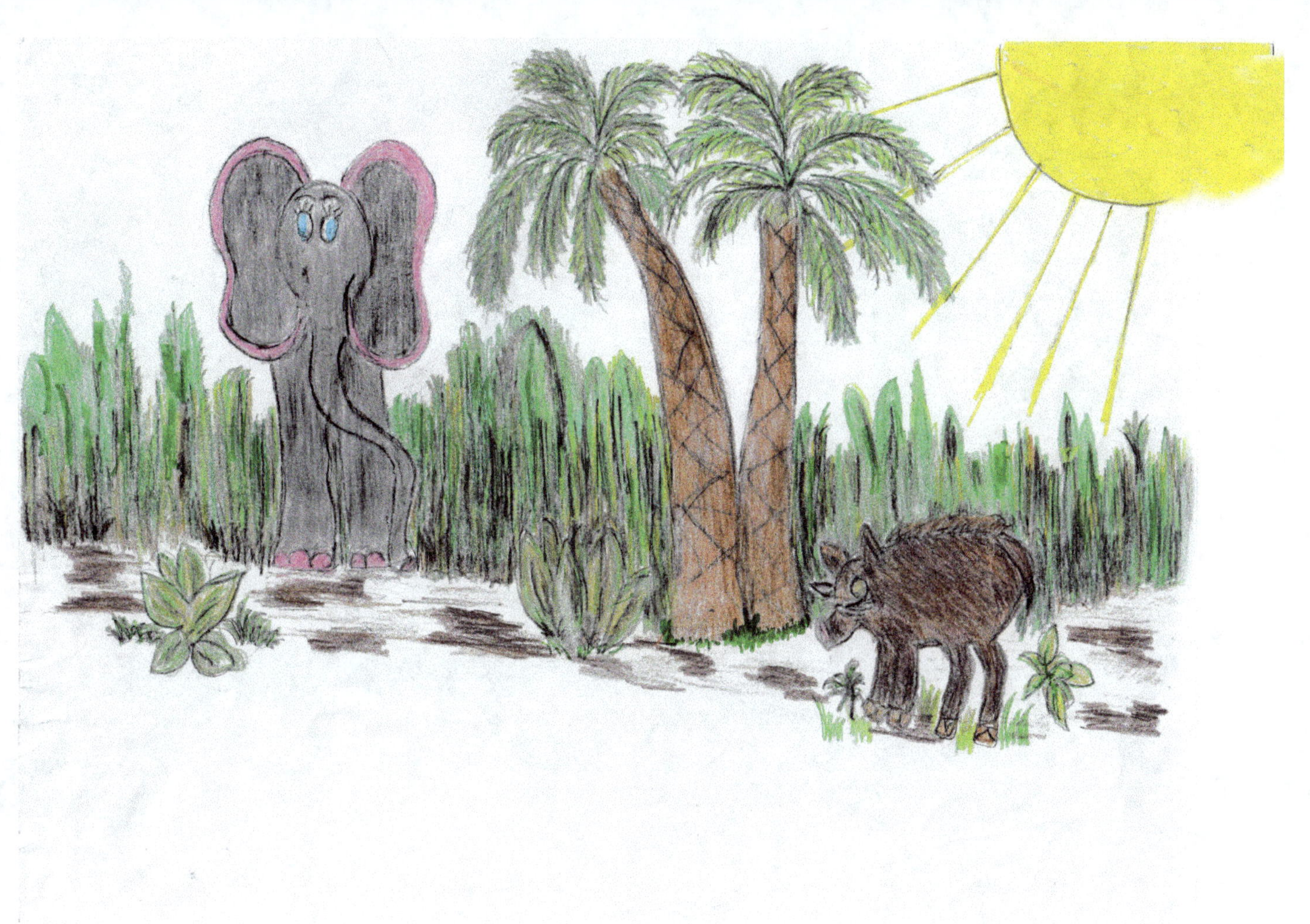

"Do you want to play with me for a while?" said Billy.

"Yes, I do," replied Little Elly.

Big Elly sat under a big tree and watched them play.

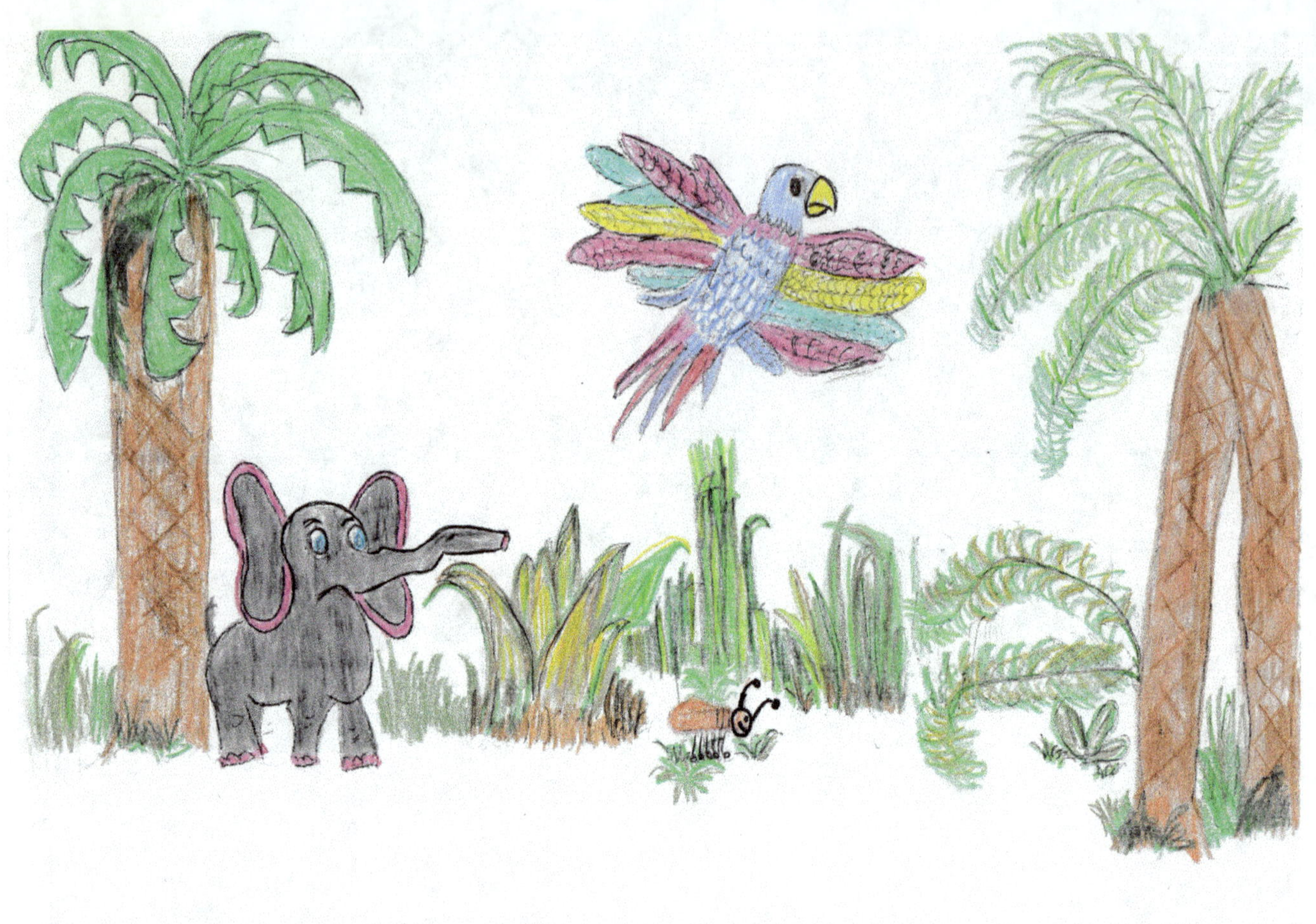

“We are going to a jungle picnic now,” said Little Elly.

“Can I come to that picnic?” chirped Polly, the parrot.

“Yes, you can,” answered Little Elly.

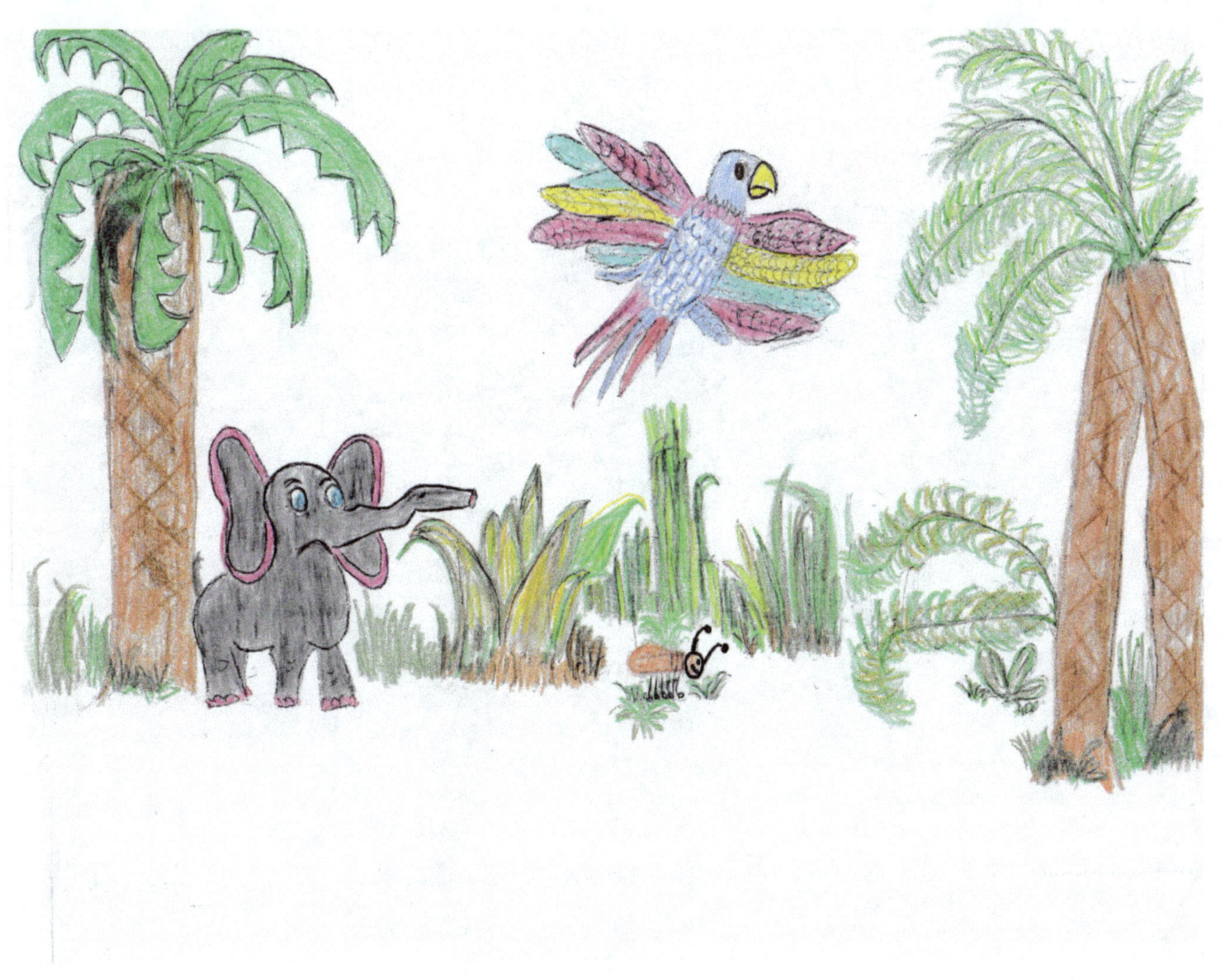

"I'm going to the picnic, too, right?" moaned Arnie, the Ant. Big Elly laughed and said "And I'm glad you're coming,

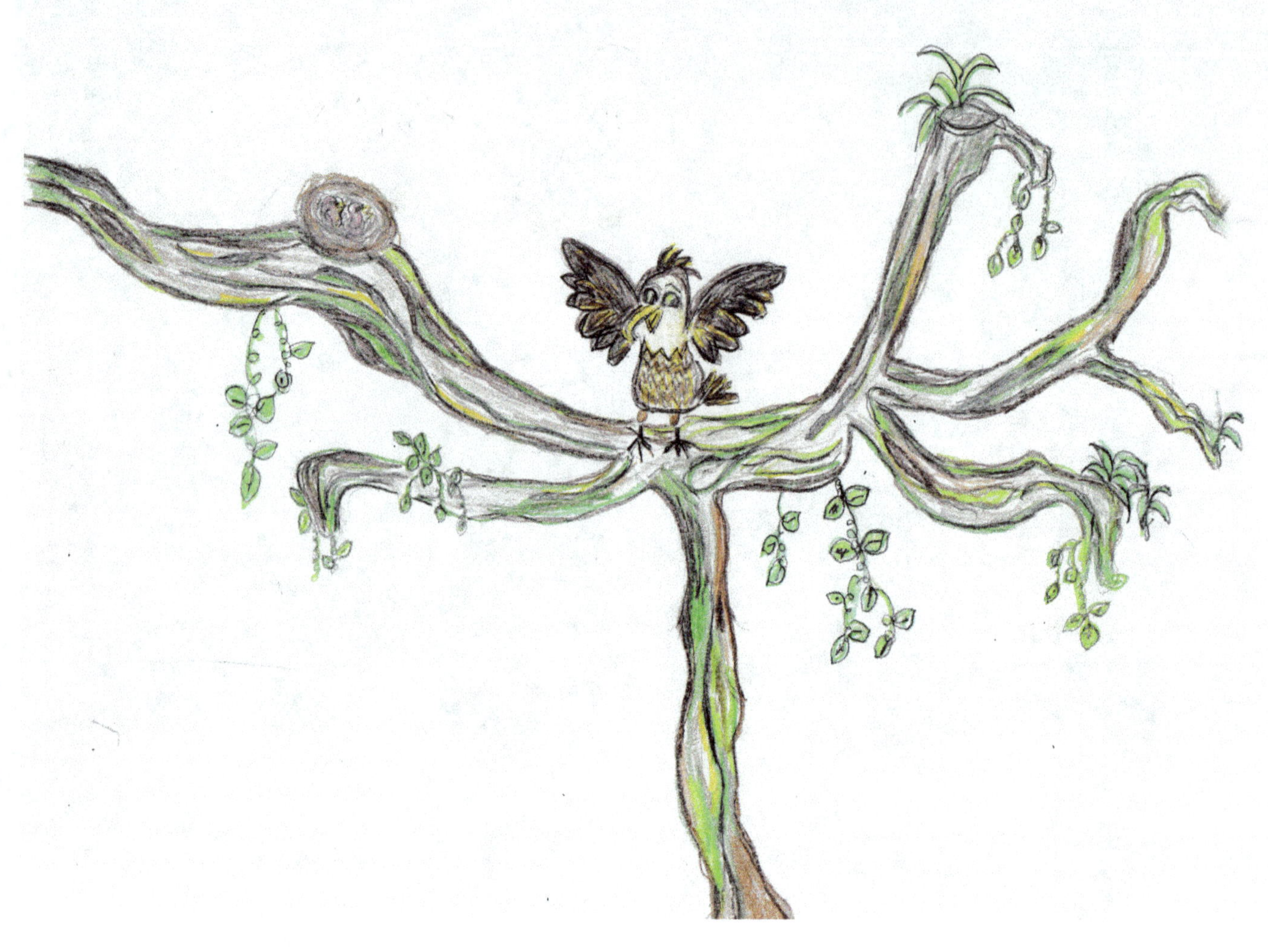

"Can I come to the picnic too?" asked Ernie, the eagle.

"Yes, you can," said Little Elly.

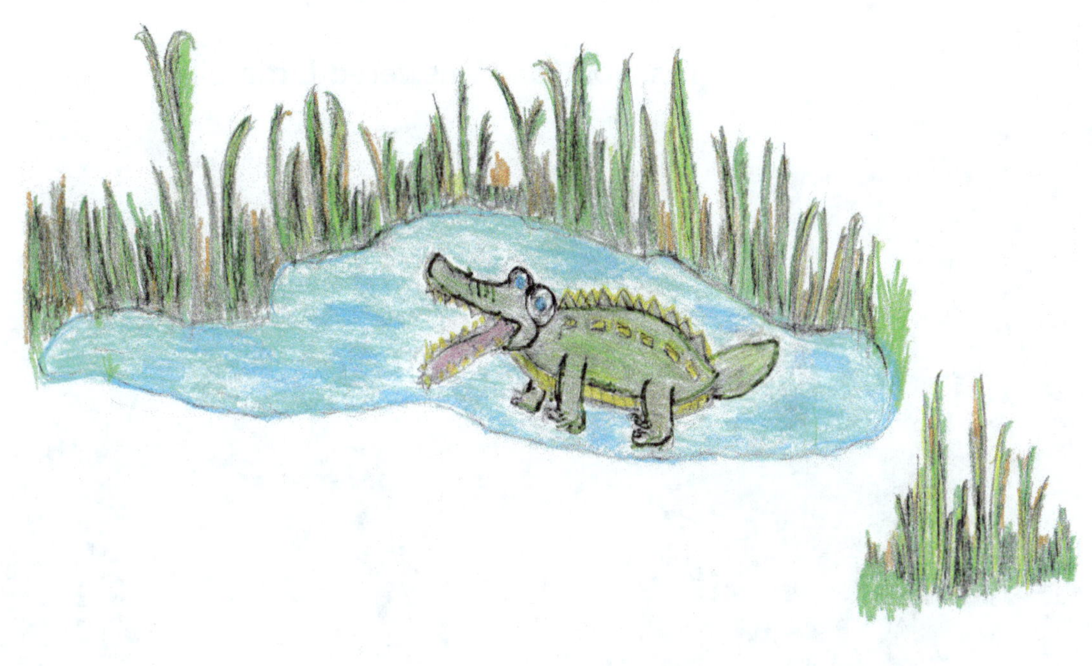

"Can I come to the picnic, too?" roared Connie, the crocodile.

"Yes, you can," said Little Elly.

“Can I come, too?” asked Gerry, the gazelle.

“Yes, you can, “answered Little Elly.

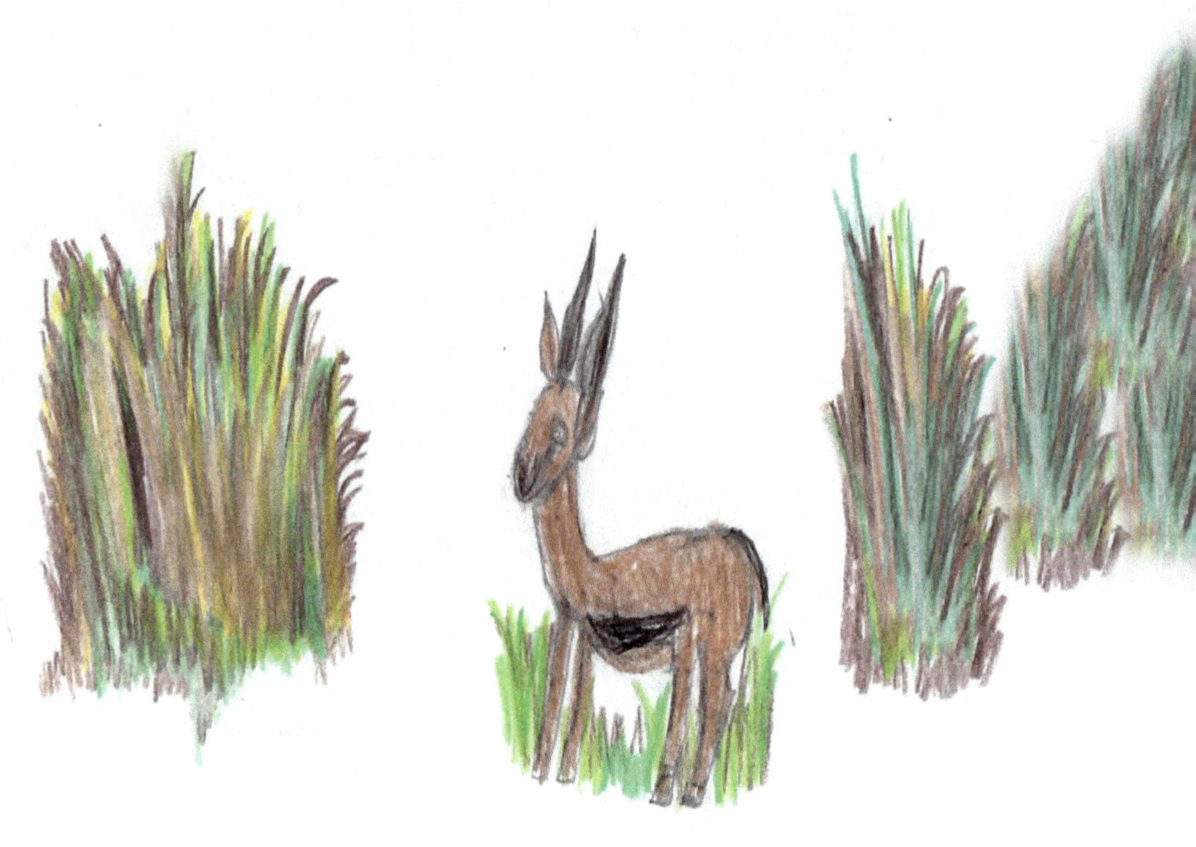

"Can I come, too?" squeaked Randy, the rat.

"Yes, you can," said Little Elly.

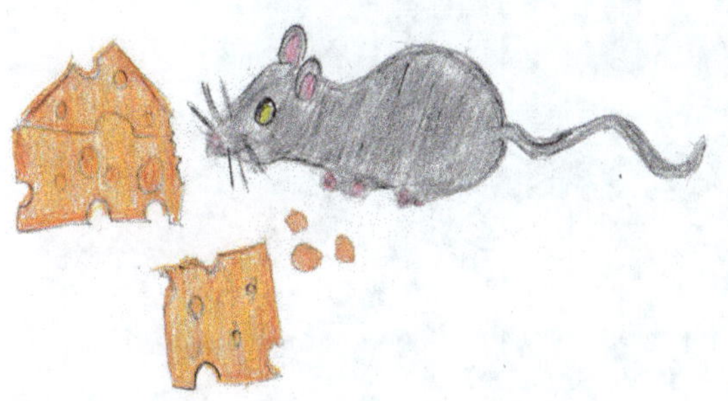

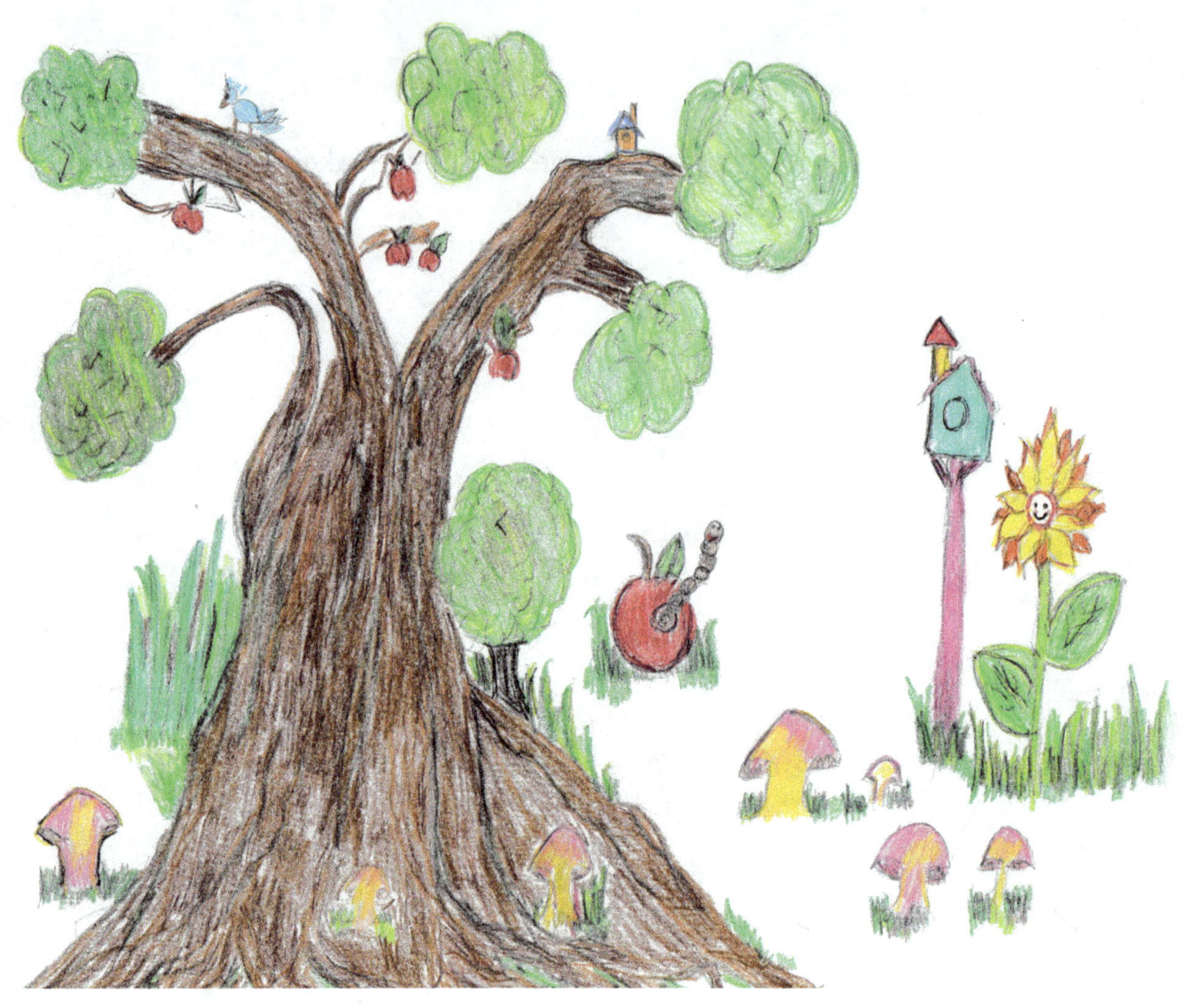

“Can I come, too?” asked Willy, the worm.

“Yes, you can, “ said Little Elly.

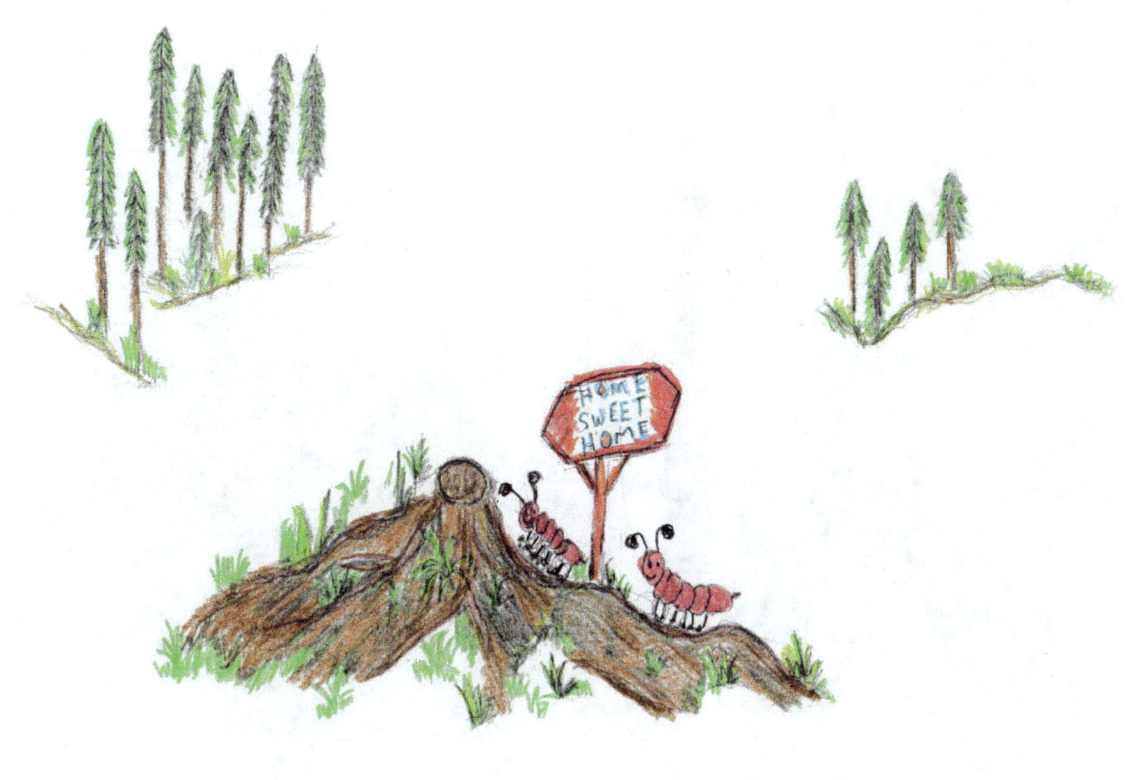

"Can we come too?" asked Amy and Alex, the ants.

"Yes, you can," said Little Elly.

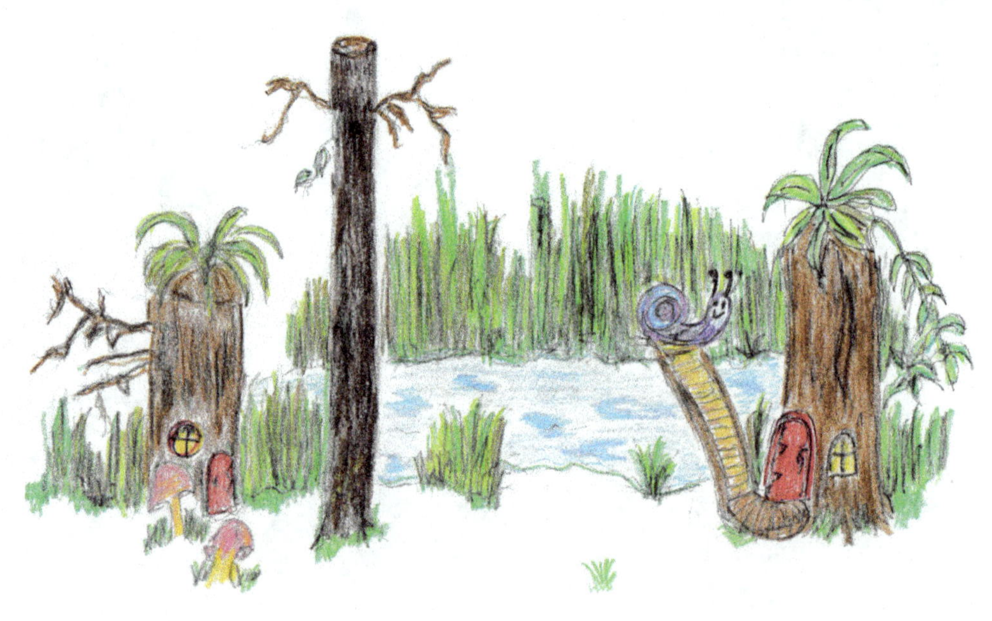

“Can I come to the picnic, too?” winced Sammy, the slug.

“Yes, you can!” replied Little Elly.

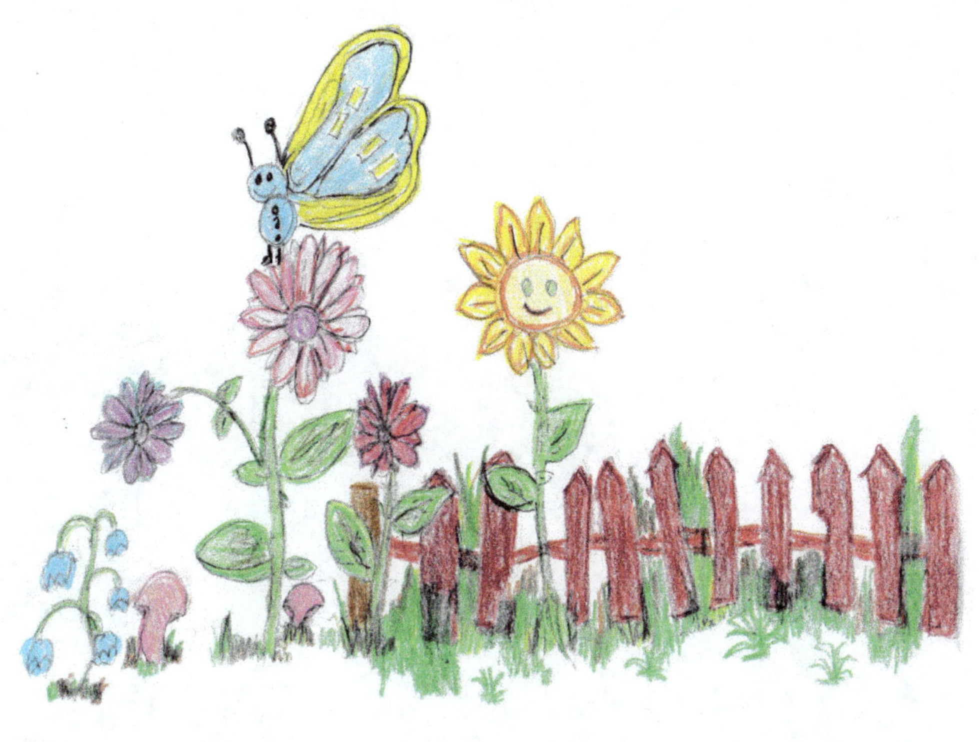

"Can I come, too?" asked Bonnie, the butterfly, as she sat on a pink flower.

"Yes, you can," said Little Elly.

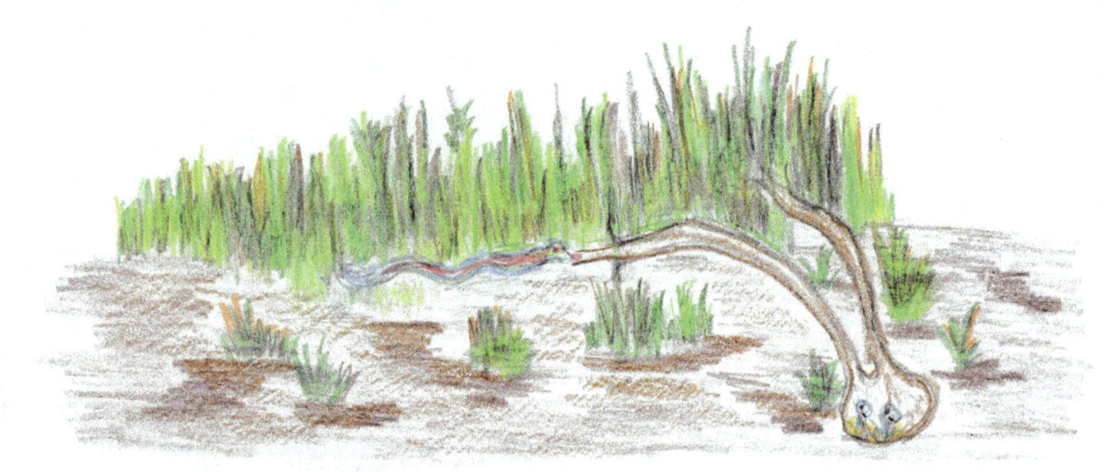

"Can I come too?" asked Simon, the snake, as he slithered through a patch of green grass.

"Yes, you can," said Little Elly.

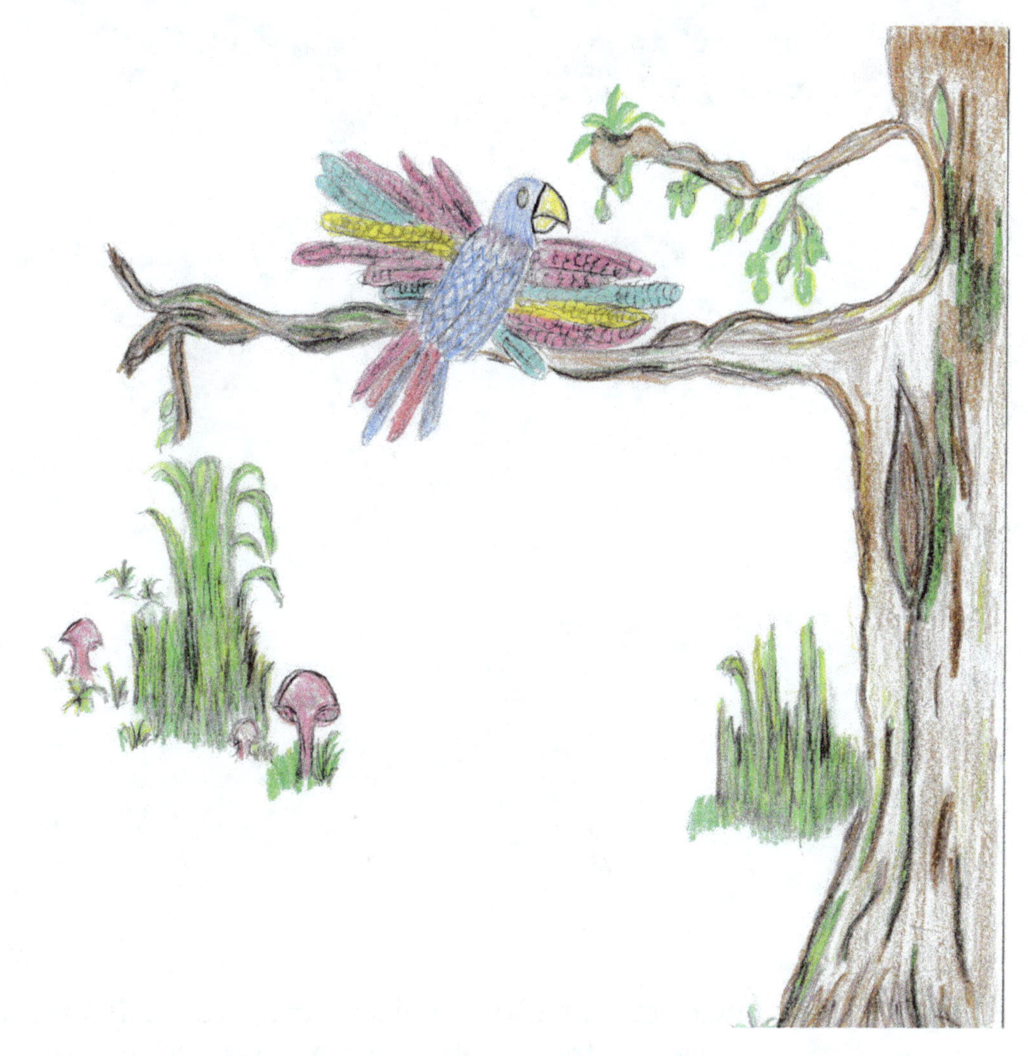

“My best friend, Polly, is going to that picnic,” said Peter, another parrot.
“Can I join in, too?”

“Yes, you can,” said Little Elly.

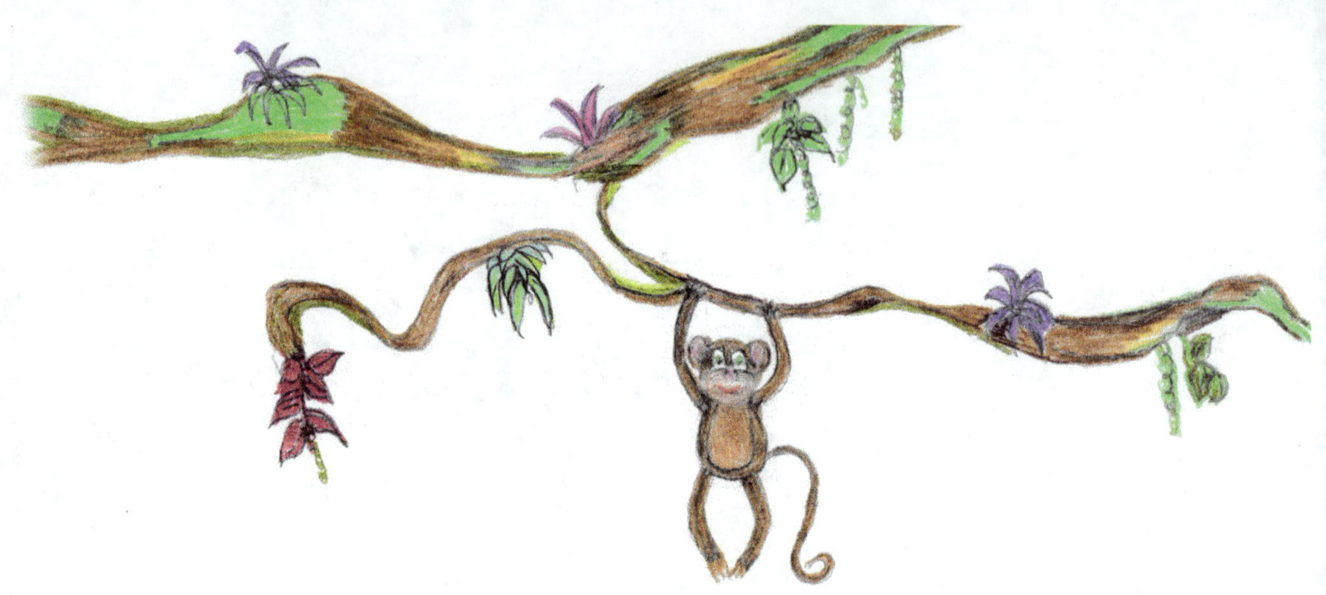

"Hey, I want to come to the picnic, too," called Moses, the monkey, as he swung through the jungle trees. "Can I come?"

"Yes, you can," answered Little Elly.

"Bring bananas, please," said Big Elly

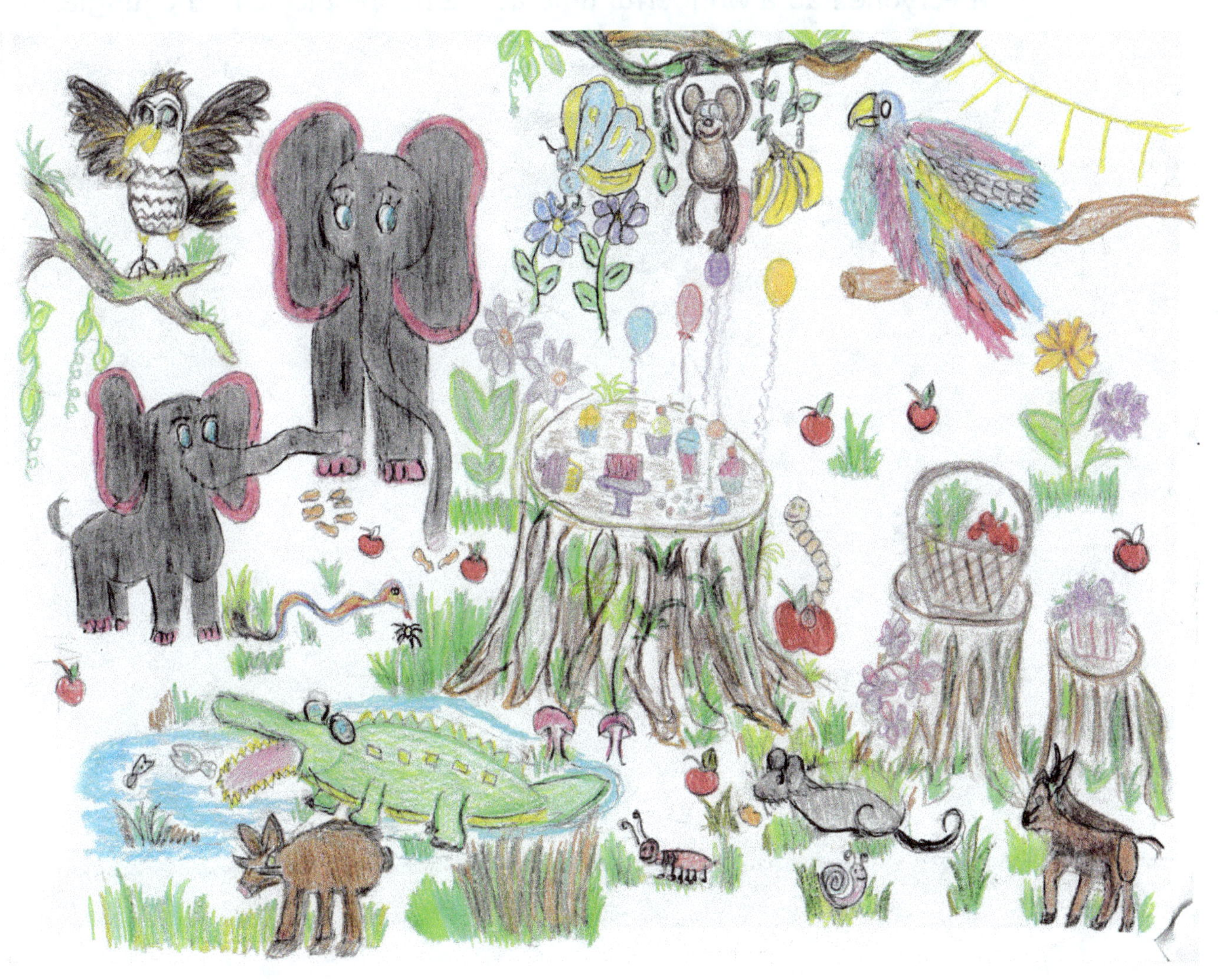

Little Elly's guests gathered in a clearing in the jungle near the river.

Big Elly and Little Elly enjoyed conversation and play with their new friends, and they shared bits of their lunches with them.

Everyone had a wonderful time at the happy picnic in the jungle.

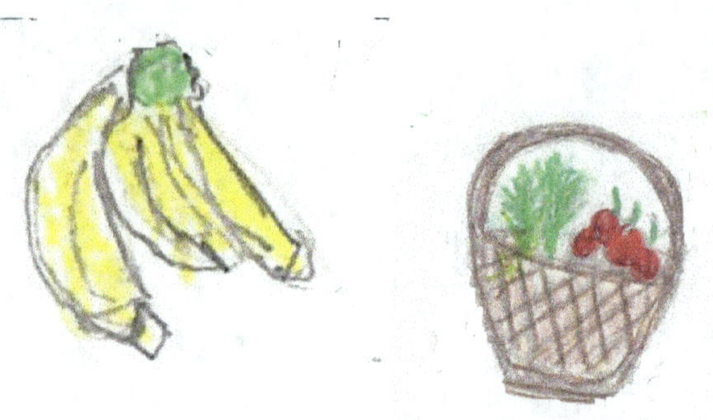

THE END

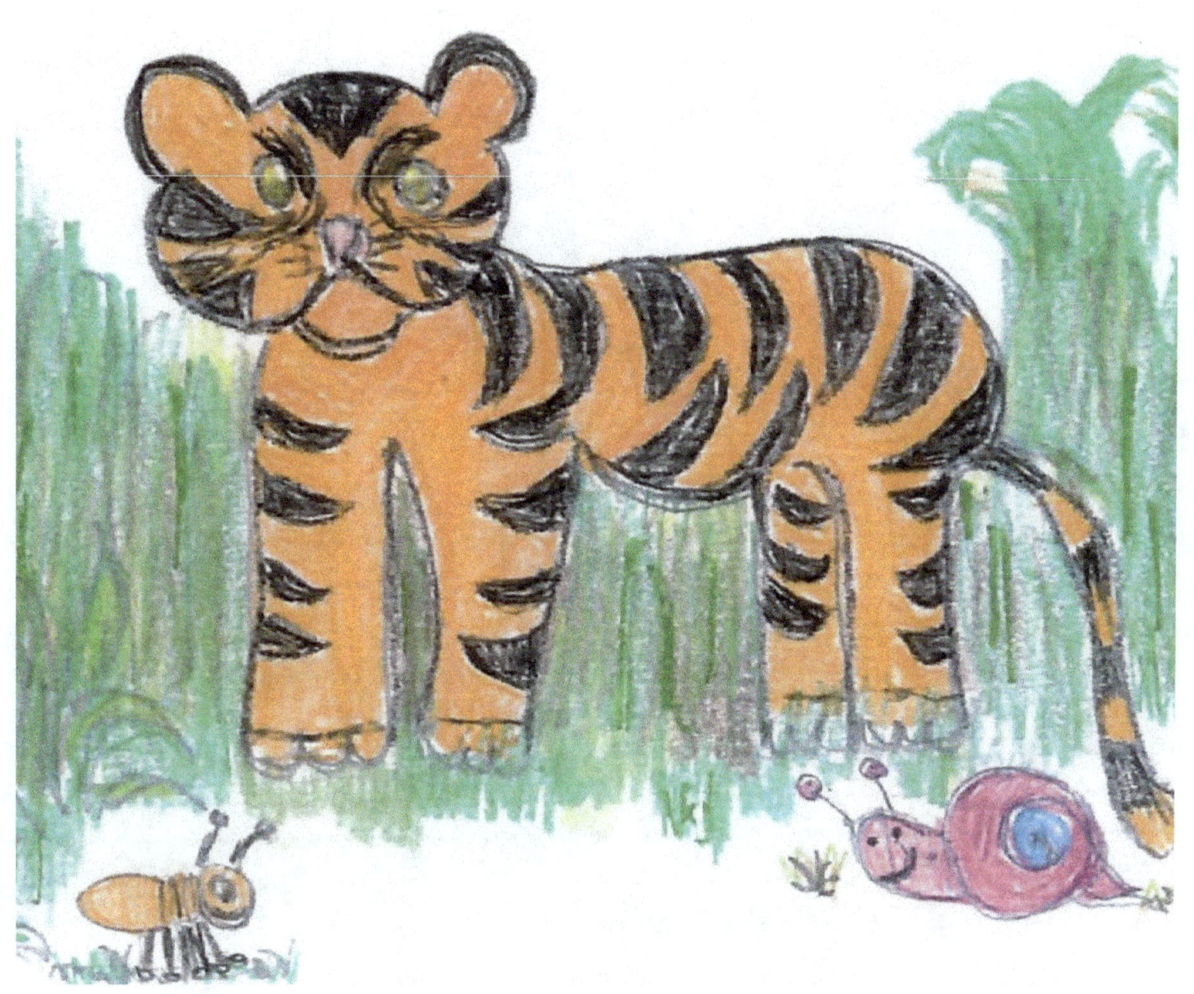

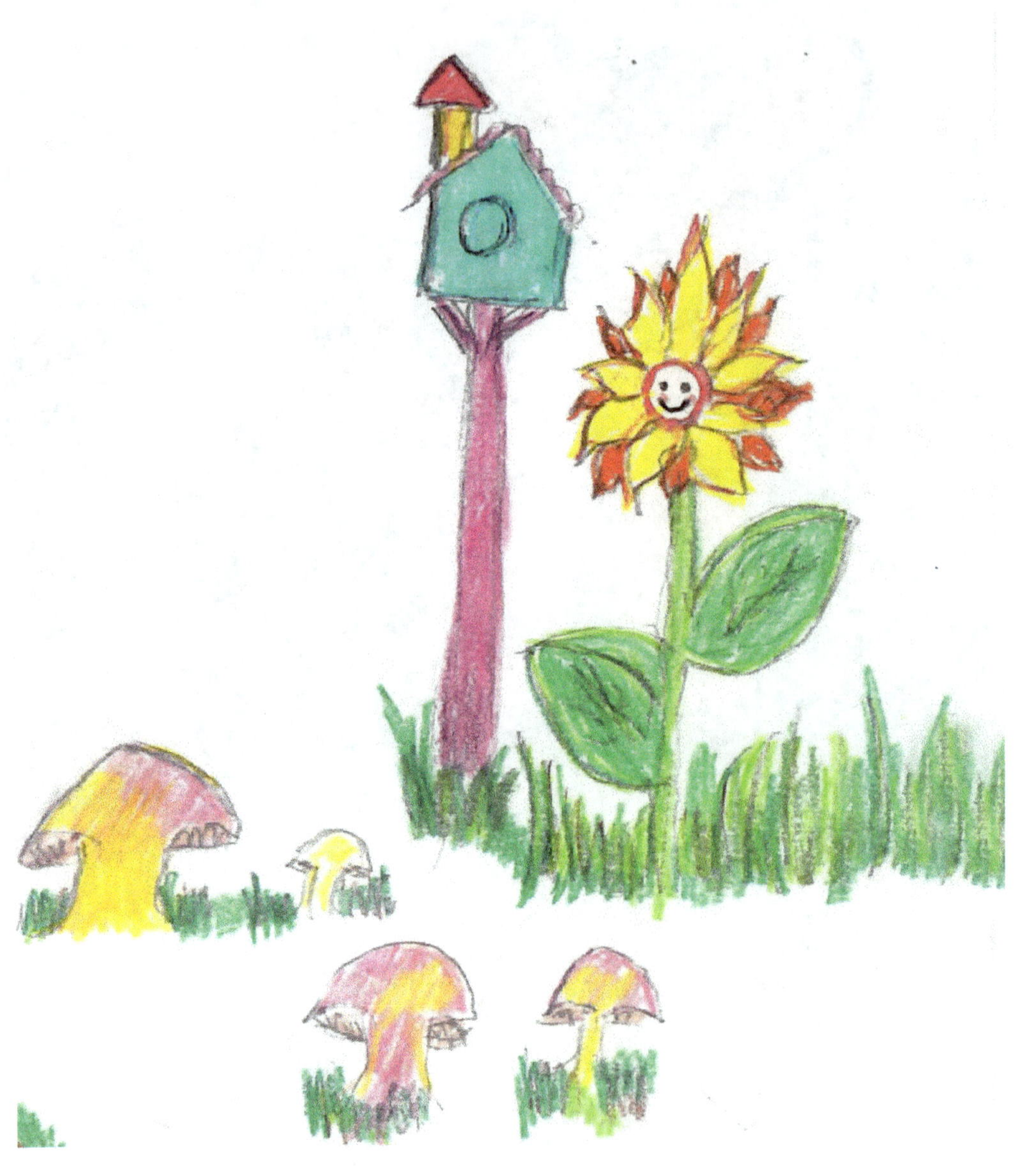

About the Author

RP Mickelson is a writer who specializes in novels and short stories about spiritual renewal and personal transformation. He also wrote a historical book about homesteading in Western Canada in the early 20th century based on the lives of his Norwegian ancestors. He's working on book three of a fictional trilogy about mystical healing.

Mr. Mickelson is now venturing into the genre of children's stories. His motivation for this endeavour is to entertain or educate any or all of his seven grandchildren through the medium of quality literature. He is delighted to partner with local artist Penny E. Ross.

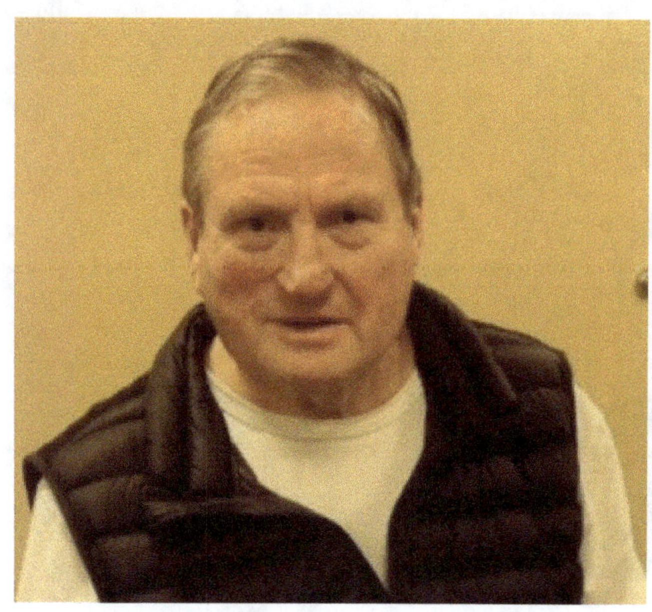

About the Illustrator

Penny E. Ross has loved drawing, doodling, sketching and painting since she was eleven years old. After her Grade 6 teacher told her she had artistic talent, Penny dreamed of becoming a professional artist one day.

In adulthood, many of her friends and relatives encouraged Penny to keep drawing, which she did with a passionate dedication to mastering her craft. Penny's paintings have been popular for some years, but this is the first publication of her illustrations.

Penny's magnificent artwork is now fully displayed in this work, and she is already working on her next book. She is delighted to join forces with well-known local author RP Mickelson as the official artist for his children's books.

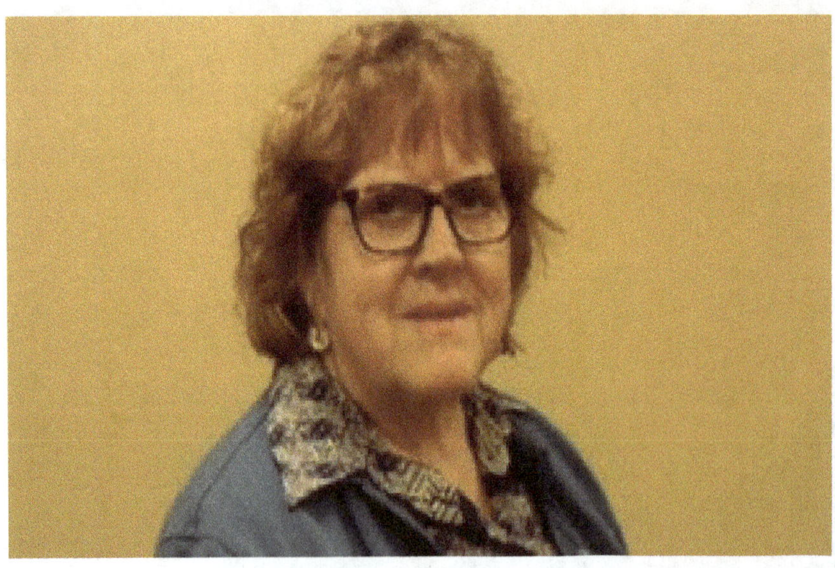

www.ingramcontent.com/pod-product-compliance
Lightning Source LLC
LaVergne TN
LVHW061205120826
845149LV00011B/1913

* 9 7 8 1 9 9 8 3 0 7 0 8 1 *